JACK
AND THE BEANSTALK

Illustrated by Rafael Mayani

BONNEY
PRESS

Published by Bonney Press,
an imprint of Hinkler Books Pty Ltd
45–55 Fairchild Street
Heatherton Victoria 3202 Australia
www.hinkler.com

BONNEY
PRESS

© Hinkler Books Pty Ltd 2016

Illustration: Rafael Mayani
Text: Katie Hewat
Design: Paul Scott and Pooja Desai
Editorial: Emily Murray

ISBN: 978 1 4889 0466 0

Printed and bound in Poland

JACK
AND THE BEANSTALK

nce upon a time there was a boy named Jack who lived in a small cottage with his mother. The only possession they had in the world was a cow named Milky-White, whose milk they sold at the market.

But one day, Milky-White stopped giving milk, and Jack's mother told him to sell her so they could get some money for food.

The next morning, on his way to the market, Jack met a strange old man who proposed a swap: Milky-White for a handful of beans.

'But they're not just any beans,' the man told Jack. *They're magic!* Jack knew he had to have them. 'If they don't grow,' the old man said, 'I'll give you your cow back and will throw in a free bag of cow manure for your trouble.' That sealed the deal – they made the exchange.

WHOOP!!!!

Once he was around the next bend, the old man let out a 'whoop!'
He couldn't believe his luck. Ever since he'd eaten one of those awful
beans he'd had *terrible* pains in his stomach. He'd been coughing up
leaves, and shoots had begun growing out of his ears.

When Jack arrived home, he proudly showed his mother the beans and told her of the special deal he had made with the old man. His mother took the beans and looked at them.

'WHAT?' she exclaimed. 'How could you be so foolish as to give away our Milky-White for a handful of beans?' And with that, she threw the beans at Jack and they bounced out the window.

To Jack's delight, when he awoke the next morning he saw that the beans had grown in the night. They had formed a beanstalk that climbed up and up until it vanished into the clouds. Jack ran to the garden to take a closer look.

'I wonder where it ends?' thought Jack. 'I bet I could easily climb it and see!' So he took a firm hold and began to climb, *higher* and *higher* into the sky.

At the top, he found himself beside a cobbled road that led to an enormous castle. Jack stood still with his mouth gaping open – he couldn't believe his luck!

'You there, *stop*!' Jack turned and saw a woman rushing towards him. 'Do not go near that castle! A **monstrous giant** lives there who has stolen many treasures from the folk who live in this land. He eats children like you for breakfast!'

Now, Jack wasn't the brightest boy in the world, and he had never been in a castle before. So he ignored the woman, and continued up the road.

When Jack arrived at the castle, he knocked on the door, and it was opened by the **biggest**, **tallest** woman Jack had ever seen. She was, in fact, a giantess.

Jack cleared his throat. 'Good morning ma'am,' he said politely. 'Would you be so kind as to spare a poor boy some breakfast?'

The giantess had always liked children, so Jack was soon sitting at her table eating porridge out of one of her thimbles. Just as he finished his last spoonful, the house began to *shake*.

'Oh, *no!*' cried the giantess. 'My husband is home, and if he finds you here, he'll eat you for breakfast. QUICK, hide in the oven!'

Before Jack could think about whether or not an oven was the best place to hide from a hungry giant, he leapt in and the door was shut behind him.

The giant thumped into the room and stopped abruptly, sniffing the air. Then he cried out in a voice like thunder:

Fee-fi-fo-fum

I smell the blood
of an Englishman!

Be he alive or be he dead,

I'll **grind** his bones
to make my bread.

'Nonsense,' said the giantess. 'It must be the man you had for dinner yesterday.' She brought him a plate of roast beef, and patted his giant head.

Once the giant had finished his meal, he got up and opened the door to an adjoining room. Jack could see, through a crack in the oven door, that the room was filled with bags of glorious, **shining** gold. The giant sat down and began to count some of the money, until eventually his head began to nod and he started to snore.

Jack crept out of the oven. As he tiptoed past the giant, he snatched a bag of gold and ran as *fast* as he could to the beanstalk. When he got home, he told his mother of his adventure and proudly showed her his loot.

'With this money we can eat well for months!' she exclaimed.
She hugged Jack tightly.

Encouraged by his mother's reaction, Jack woke the next morning and climbed the beanstalk again. Once he reached the top, he ran past the woman (as she tried, again, to warn the silly boy), went straight to the castle door and knocked.

Soon Jack was sitting at the table, while the giantess smiled and watched him eat his porridge. But **again**, as he finished his breakfast, the house began to tremble. Jack quickly scrambled into the oven, just as the giant stomped in. The giant bellowed:

Fee-fi-fo-fum

I smell the blood of an Englishman!

Be he alive or be he dead,

I'll **grind** his bones

to make my bread.

But the giantess just chuckled and gave the giant some chicken nuggets.

Afterwards, the giant left the kitchen for a moment and came back holding a hen. The giant placed the hen and her nest on the table and said, 'LAY.'

Miraculously, the hen did as she was told and laid an egg made entirely of gold. After patting the hen and smiling at the egg for quite some time, the giant's head began to nod and he started to snore.

SNOORRRE

Quick as a flash, Jack crept out of the oven, grabbed hold of the hen and the golden egg, and climbed as fast as he could down the beanstalk.

When he got home, he proudly showed his mother the giant hen and she marvelled at the magnificent, **solid-gold** egg.

The next morning Jack was up the beanstalk before the sun had risen.

Once again, as Jack was eating porridge, the house began to *shake* and Jack climbed into the oven. The giant came in, bellowed something about an Englishman and ate his lamb wrap.

Then he got up and left the room for a moment, returning with a beautiful antique harp.

The giant put the harp on the table and said, *'Sing!'* At once, the golden harp came to life and began to sing beautifully. It sang until the giant's head began to nod and he began to snore.

Master, Master!

Jack crept out of the oven and snatched the harp from in front of the sleeping giant. But as he did, the harp cried out, 'Master, Master!' and the giant instantly awoke.

Jack ran as fast as he could back to the beanstalk, with the giant close behind. He scrambled down quickly and when he reached the bottom, his mother grabbed an axe and hacked at the beanstalk until it came tumbling down. The terrifying giant came crashing down with it, never to eat any Englishmen or steal from anyone ever again.

Scared out of his wits, Jack promised his mother that he would never make silly market deals again.

But one day, on his way to the market to sell his golden eggs and show his golden harp, Jack met a strange old man who made him an irresistible offer. And, in exchange for his hen and his harp, Jack became the proud owner of a horse that the old man assured him could fly.